For The Mean Groovers,
and also Carey, Lloyd and Dizzy

Copyright © 1992 by Peter O'Donnell.
All rights reserved. Published by Scholastic Inc.,
by arrangement with ABC, All Books for Children,
33 Museum Street, London WC1A 1LD, England.

Library of Congress Cataloging-in-Publication Data
O'Donnell, Peter.
Dizzy / by Peter O'Donnell
p.   cm.
Summary: Left behind at the airport, an elephant searches
for his friends in what seems to be a concrete jungle.
ISBN 0-590-45475-7
[1. Elephants—Fiction. 2. Airports—Fiction.] I. Title.
PZ7.02245Di   1992   91-36825
[E]—dc20   CIP
                                                              AC

12 11 10 9 8 7 6 5 4 3 2 1   2 3 4 5 6 7/9
Printed in Hong Kong
First Scholastic printing, September 1992

Dizzy

PETER O'DONNELL

SCHOLASTIC INC. · NEW YORK

Life in the jungle was not as peaceful as it used to be for Dizzy and his friends. Tourists came from all over the world to visit and take pictures of the animals.

One day, after the tourists had left to have dinner, Dizzy found a little boy wandering by himself. Dizzy picked him up, and he and his friends took the boy to the nearest village.

Sure enough, the little boy's parents were searching all over for him and, to show their gratitude, his father promised he would take Dizzy and his friends to see where they lived.

The little boy's father owned an airline,
which was a good thing, because Dizzy and
his friends needed a whole plane to themselves.
Everyone enjoyed the movie *Tarzan*, which
was shown especially for them.

They landed near a big city and waited patiently for their suitcases. Then a man came to take them to the biggest car they had ever seen. It was a stretch limousine.

Everyone piled in but, in the excitement, no one noticed that Dizzy had gotten stuck in the automatic doors. He was just too big. He tried calling to his friends, but there was so much noise from the planes and the people that they didn't hear him.

Dizzy watched as his friends drove off.

Finally, a woman complained that an elephant
was blocking the doors. All of the people stuck
behind Dizzy pushed, and all the people in front
of Dizzy pulled until he popped out of the doors.

Dizzy was too big for a taxi so he took
a bus into the city to search for his friends.

When Dizzy reached the city,
he walked along streets and
across bridges, took a boat
on the river . . .

. . . and an elevator up a tower, but he didn't see his friends anywhere.

It was getting dark; cars whizzed by, and
shadows were cast from the streetlights.

Dizzy was tired. He'd had a long day. At
last he found a quiet street, sat down and
fell asleep. In his sleep he dreamed the
dreams that elephants dream.

Dizzy awoke to the harsh sounds
of the big city. It was morning, and
there were cars and buses and trucks
everywhere. There was a traffic jam,
and Dizzy was in the middle of it.
In fact, Dizzy *was* the traffic jam.
But he was surrounded, and
he couldn't move.

Suddenly, Dizzy heard a whirring sound above his head. A helicopter! With all his friends! The pilot lowered a harness, and Dizzy put it on. Then Dizzy was rescued. Everyone chattered at once, and Dizzy learned that the little boy he'd rescued had seen him on the television news and told his father.

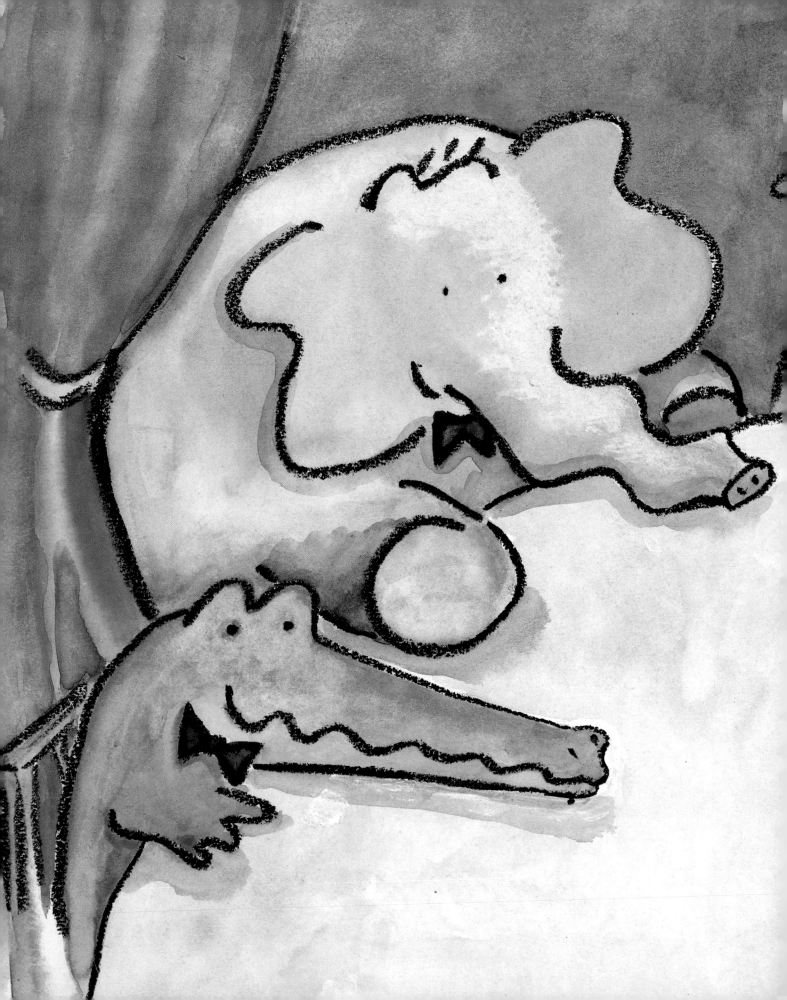

Dizzy got to ride
in the stretch limousine,
and he and his friends
all ate dinner in a fancy
restaurant before flying home.
   The little boy and his father
invited Dizzy back, anytime, but
Dizzy politely said no. He had
decided that he preferred his
jungle to their concrete one.